# CUPID AND PSYCHE

Translated (A.D. 1566)

from the Latin of Apuleius

BY

WILLIAM ADLINGTON

With Twelve Photogravures after Drawings by

GILBERT JAMES

British Library Cataloguing-in-Publication Data
A catalogue record for this book is available from the
British Library

# Greek Mythology

Greek mythology is the body of myths and teachings that belong to the ancient Greeks, concerning their gods and heroes, the nature of the world, and the origins and significance of their own cult and ritual practices. It was a part of the religion in ancient Greece. Modern scholars refer to and study the myths in an attempt to throw light on the religious and political institutions of Ancient Greece and its civilization, and to gain understanding of the nature of myth-making itself.

Greek mythology is explicitly embodied in a large collection of narratives, and implicitly in Greek representational arts, such as vase-paintings and votive gifts; it attempts to explain the origins of the world, and details the lives and adventures of a wide variety of gods, goddesses, heroes, heroines, and mythological creatures. These accounts were originally disseminated in an oral-poetic tradition, but today the Greek myths are known primarily from Greek literature.

The oldest known Greek literary sources, Homer's epic poems *Iliad* and *Odyssey*, focus on the Trojan War and its aftermath. Other poets completed the 'epic cycle', but these later and lesser poems now are lost almost entirely. Two poems by Homer's near contemporary Hesiod, the *Theogony* and the *Works and Days*, contain accounts of the genesis of the world, the succession of divine rulers, the succession of human ages, the origin of human woes, and the origin of sacrificial practices. This work is perhaps the fullest account of the earliest Greek myths, as well as an elaborate genealogy and collection of folk tales. *Works and Days*, a didactic poem about farming life, also includes the myths of Prometheus, Pandora, and the Five Ages, also containing Hesiod's advice on the best way to succeed in a dangerous world, rendered yet more dangerous by its gods. Myths are also preserved in the Homeric Hymns, in fragments of epic poems of the 'epic cycle', lyric poems, in the works of the tragedians of the fifth century BC, in writings of scholars and poets of the Hellenistic Age, and in texts from the time of the Roman Empire by writers such as Plutarch and Pausanias. Despite their traditional name, the 'Homeric Hymns' have no direct connection with Homer however. They are choral hymns from the earlier part of the so-called Lyric age.

Mythical narration plays an important role in nearly every genre of Greek literature. Nevertheless, the only general mythographical handbook to survive from Greek antiquity was the *Library* of Pseudo-Apollodorus, a scholar who lived from c. 180 – 125 BC. This work attempts to reconcile the contradictory tales of the poets and provides a grand summary of traditional Greek mythology and heroic legends. His writings may have formed the basis for the collection, however the 'Library' discusses events that occurred long after his death, hence the name Pseudo-Apollodorus. Archaeological findings provide a principal source of detail about Greek mythology, with gods and heroes featured prominently in the decoration of many artefacts. Geometric designs on pottery of the eighth century BC depict scenes from the Trojan cycle as well as the adventures of Heracles. In the succeeding Archaic, Classical, and Hellenistic periods, Homeric and various other mythological scenes appear, supplementing the existing literary evidence. These visual representations of myths are important for two reasons. For one, many Greek myths are attested on vases earlier than in literary sources: of the twelve labours of Heracles, for example, only the <u>Cerberus</u> adventure occurs in a contemporary literary text. In addition, visual sources sometimes represent myths or mythical scenes that are not attested in any extant literary source. In some cases, the first known representation of a myth in geometric art predates its first known representation in late archaic poetry, by several centuries.

Greek mythology has had an extensive influence on the culture, arts and literature of Western civilization and remains part of Western heritage and language. Poets and artists from ancient times to the present have derived inspiration from Greek mythology and have discovered contemporary significance and relevance in the themes. The widespread adoption of Christianity did not curb the popularity of the myths. With the rediscovery of classical antiquity in the Renaissance, the poetry of Ovid became a major influence on the imagination of poets, dramatists, musicians and artists. From the early years of Renaissance, artists such as Leonardo da Vinci, Michelangelo and Raphael, portrayed the Pagan subjects of Greek mythology alongside more conventional Christian themes. In Northern Europe, Greek mythology never took the same hold of the visual arts, but its effect was very obvious on literature. The English imagination was fired by Greek mythology starting with Chaucer and John Milton and continuing through Shakespeare to Robert Bridges in the twentieth century.

Although during the Enlightenment of the eighteenth century, reaction against Greek myth spread throughout Europe, the myths continued to provide an important source of raw material for dramatists, including those who wrote the libretti for many of Handel's and Mozart's operas. By the end of the eighteenth century, Romanticism initiated a surge of enthusiasm for all things Greek, including Greek mythology. In Britain, new translations of Greek tragedies and Homer inspired contemporary poets (such as Alfred Lord Tennyson, Keats, Byron and Shelley) and painters (such as Lord Leighton and Lawrence Alma-Tadema). Christoph Gluck, Richard Strauss, Jacques Offenbach and many others set Greek mythological themes to music. In more recent times, classical themes have been reinterpreted by dramatists Jean Anouilh, Jean Cocteau, and Jean Giraudoux in France, Eugene O'Neill in America, and T. S. Eliot in Britain and by novelists such as James Joyce and André Gide. The impact and importance of Greek mythology is simply enormous, and it is hoped that the reader enjoys this book.

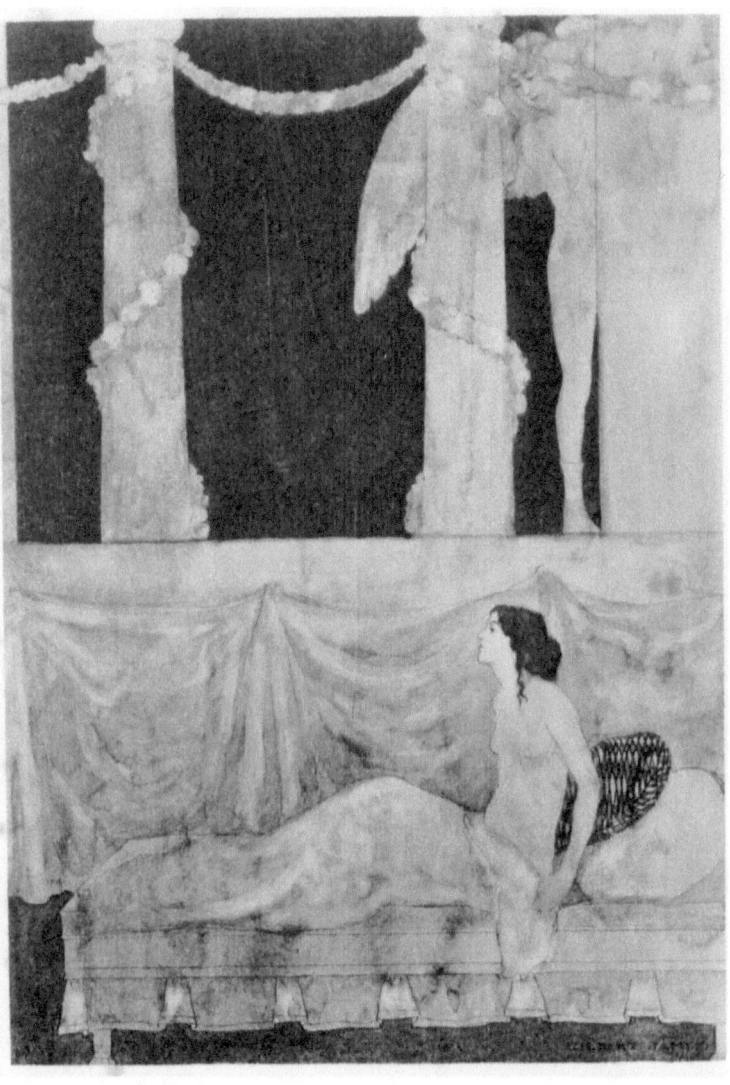

# LIST OF PHOTOGRAVURES

# THE MOST PLEASANT AND DE-LECTABLE TALE OF THE MARRIAGE OF CUPID AND PSYCHE

THERE was sometimes a certain King in-
habiting in the west parts, who had a wife a
noble Dame, by whom he had three daughters
exceeding fair, of whom the two elder were of such
comely shape and beauty as they did excel and pass
all other women living; whereby they were thought
worthily to deserve the praise and commendation of
every person, and deservedly to be preferred above
the residue of the common sort; yet the singular
passing beauty and maidenly majesty of the youngest
daughter did so far surmount and excel them two as

no earthly creature could by any means sufficiently express or set out the same.

By reason whereof, after the fame of this excellent maiden was spread abroad in every part of the city, the citizens and strangers there, being inwardly pricked by zealous affection to behold her famous person, came daily by thousands, hundreds, and scores, to her father's palace ; who, astonished with admiration of her incomparable beauty, did no less worship and reverence her with crosses, signs, and tokens, and other divine adorations, according to the custom of the old used rites and ceremonies, than if she were Lady Venus indeed.

And shortly after the fame was spread into the next cities and bordering regions that the Goddess whom the deep seas had borne and brought forth and the froth or the spurging waves had nourished, to the intent to show her high magnificence and divine power on earth to such as erst did honour and worship her, was now conversant amongst mortal men; or else that the earth and not the seas, by a new concourse and influence of the celestial planets, had budded and yielded forth a new Venus endowed with the flower of virginity.

So daily more and more increased this opinion, and now is her flying fame dispersed into the next Island and well-nigh into every part and province of the whole world. Whereupon innumerable strangers resorted from far countries, adventuring themselves by long journeys on land and by great perils on water, to behold this glorious Virgin.

By occasion whereof such a contempt grew towards the Goddess Venus that no person travelled unto the town Paphos, nor to the Isle Gindos,

nor to Cythera, to worship her. Her ornaments
were thrown out, her temples defaced, her pillows
and quishions torn, her ceremonies neglected, her
images and statues uncrowned, and her bare altars
unswept, and foul with the ashes of old burned
sacrifice. For why, every person honoured and
worshipped this maiden instead of Venus; and in the
morning at her first coming abroad offered unto
her oblations, provided banquets, called her by the
name of Venus which was not Venus indeed, and
in her honour presented flowers and garlands in
most reverent fashion.

This sudden change and alteration of celestial
honour did greatly inflame and kindle the mind of
very Venus, who, unable to temper herself from
indignation, shaking her head in raging- sort,
reasoned with herself in this manner:

"Behold the original parent of all these elements—behold the Lady Venus renounced throughout all the world, with whom a mortal maiden is joined now partaker of honour; my name, registered in the city of heaven, is profaned and made vile by terrene absurdities. If I shall suffer any mortal creature to present my majesty on earth, or that any shall hear about a false surmised shape of my person, then in vain did Paris, that shepherd in whose just judgment and confidence the great Jupiter had affiance, prefer me above the residue of the Goddesses for the excellence of my beauty. But she, whatsoever she be that hath usurped mine honour, shall shortly repent her of her unlawful estate."

And by and by she called her winged son Cupid, rash enough and hardy, who by his evil manners contemning all public justice and law, armed with

9

fire and arrows, running up and down in the nights from house to house and corrupting the lawful marriages of every person, doth nothing but that which is evil; who, although that he were of his own proper nature sufficient prone to work mischief, yet she egged him forward with words and brought him to the city, and showed him Psyche (for so the maiden was called), and having told the cause of her anger, not without great rage:

"I pray thee (quoth she), my dear child, by motherly bond of love, by the sweet wounds of thy piercing darts, by the pleasant heat of thy fire, revenge the injury which is done to thy mother, by the false and disobedient beauty of a mortal maiden, and I pray thee without delay that she may fall in love with the most miserable creature living, the most poor, the most crooked, and the most vile, that there may be none found in all the world of like wretchedness."

When she had spoken these words, she embraced and kissed her son, and took her voyage towards the sea.

When she was come to the sea, she began to call the Gods and Goddesses who were obedient at her voice. For incontinent came the daughters of Nereus singing with tunes melodiously—Portunus with his bristled and rough beard; Salatia with her bosom full of fish; Palemon the driver of the Dolphin; the trumpeters of Triton leaping hither and thither and blowing with heavenly noise: such was the company which followed Venus marching towards the ocean sea.

In the mean season Psyche with all her beauty received no fruit of her honour. She was wondered at of all; she was praised of all; but she perceived that no king nor prince nor any of the inferior sort did repair to' woo her. Every one marvelled at her divine beauty, as it were at some image well painted and set out.

Her other two sisters, which were nothing so greatly exalted by the people, were royally married to two kings; but the virgin Psyche sitting at home alone lamented her solitary life, and being disquieted both in mind and body, although she pleased all the world, yet hated she in herself her own beauty.

Whereupon the miserable father of this unfortunate daughter, suspecting that the Gods and powers of heaven did envy her estate, went into the town called Miletus to receive the oracle of Apollo, where he made his prayers and offered sacrifice, and desired a husband for his daughter; but Apollo,

12

though he were a Grecian and of the country of
Ionia, because of the foundation of Miletus, yet he
gave answer in Latin verse, the sense whereof
was this :

> Let Psyche's corpse be clad in mourning weed
>   And set on rock on yonder hill aloft ;
> Her husband is no weight of human seed,
>   But serpent dire and fierce, as may be thought,
> Who flies with wings above in starry skies,
>   And doth subdue each thing with fiery flight.
> The Gods themselves and powers that seem so wise
>   With mighty love be subject to his might.
> The rivers black and deadly floods of pain
>   And darkness eke as thrall to him remain.

The King sometimes happy, when he heard the
prophecy of Apollo returned home sad and sorrowful,
and declared to his wife the miserable and unhappy
fate of his daughter; then they began to lament,

and weep, and passed over many days in great
sorrow.

But now the time approached of Psyche's
marriage: preparation was made, black torches
were lighted, and pleasant songs were turned into
pitiful cries, the melody of Hymen was ended with
deadly howling, the maiden that should be married
did wipe her eyes with her veil; all the family and
people of the city weeped likewise, and with great
lamentation was ordained a remiss time for that
day, but necessity compelled that Psyche should be
brought to her appointed place according to the
divine commandment.

And when the solemnity was ended, they went
to bring this sorrowful spouse not to her marriage,
but to her final end and burial. And while the father
and mother of Psyche did go forward, weeping and

crying to do this enterprise, Psyche spake unto them
in this sort:

"Why torment you your unhappy age with
continual dolour?   Why trouble you your spirits,
which are more rather mine than yours?   Why soil
ye your faces with tears, which I ought to adore and
worship?   Why tear you my eyes in yours?   Why
pull you your hoary hairs?   Why knock you your
breasts for me?   Now you see the reward of my
excellent beauty;   now, now, you perceive, but too
late, the plague of envy.   When the people did
honour me and call me New Venus, then you should
have wept—then you should have sorrowed, as
though I had been then dead.   For now I see and
perceive that I am come to this misery by the only
name of Venus.   Bring me, and as fortune hath
appointed, place me on the top of the rock: I greatly

desire to end my marriage; I greatly covet to see my husband. Why do I delay? Why should I refuse him that is appointed to destroy all the world?

Thus ended she her words, and thrust herself amongst the people that followed. Then they brought her to the appointed rock of the high hill, and set her thereon, and so departed. The torches and lights were put out with the tears of the people; and, every man gone home, the miserable parents, well-nigh consumed with sorrow, gave themselves to everlasting darkness.

Thus poor Psyche, being left alone weeping and trembling on the top of the rock, was blown by the gentle air and of shrilling Zephyrus, and carried from the hill with a meek wind, which retained her garments up, and by little and little brought her

down into a deep valley, where she was laid in a bed
of most sweet and fragrant flowers.

Thus fair Psyche, being sweetly couched amongst
the soft and tender herbs as in a bed of sote and
fragrant flowers, and having qualified the troubles
and thoughts of her restless mind, was now well
reposed.

And when she had refreshed herself sufficiently
with sleep, she rose with a more quiet and pacified
mind, and fortuned to espy a pleasant wood
environed with great and mighty trees.

She espied likewise a running river as clear as
crystal: in the midst of the wood, well-nigh at the
fall of the river, was a princely edifice, wrought and
builded not by the art or hand of man but by the
mighty power of God; and you would judge at the
first entry therein that it were some pleasant and

worthy mansion for the powers of heaven. For the embowings above were of cytern and ivory, propped and undermined with pillars of gold; the walls covered and seeled with silver; divers sorts of beasts were graven and carved, that seemed to encounter with such as entered in : all things were so curiously and finely wrought that it seemed either to be the work of some demi-god or God himself.

The pavement was all of precious stone, divided and cut one from another, whereon was carved divers kinds of pictures in such sort that blessed and thrice blessed were they which might go upon such a pavement; every part and angle of the house was so well adorned that, by reason of the precious stones and inestimable treasure there, it glittered and shone in such sort that the chambers, porches and doors, gave light as it had been the sun.

Neither otherwise did the other treasure of the house disagree unto so great a majesty, that verily it seemed in every point a heavenly palace fabricate and builded for Jupiter himself.

Then Psyche, moved with delectation, approached nigh, and taking a bold heart entered into the house, and beheld everything there with great affection: she saw storehouses wrought exceeding fine and replenished with abundance of riches. Finally there could nothing be devised which lacked there; but amongst such great store of treasure this was more marvellous, that there was no closure, bolt, nor lock, to keep the same.

And when with great pleasure she viewed all these things, she heard a voice without any body that said:

"Why do you marvel, madame, at so great riches?

Behold all that you see is at your commandment: wherefore go you into the chamber and repose yourself upon the bed, and desire what bath you will have; and we whose voices you hear be your servants and ready to minister unto you according to your desire. In the mean season royal meats and dainty dishes shall be prepared for you."

Then Psyche perceived the felicity of divine providence, and, according to the advertisement of the incorporal voices, she first reposed herself upon the bed, and then refreshed her body in the bains. This done, she saw the table garnished with meats, and a chair to sit down.

When Psyche was set down, all sorts of divine meats and wines were brought in, not by anybody but as it were with a wind, for she could see no person before her, but only hear voices on every side.

After that all the services were brought to the table, one came in and sang invisibly, another played on the harp, but she saw no man. The harmony of the instruments did so greatly thrill in her ears that, though there were no manner of person, yet seemed she in the midst of a multitude of people.

All these pleasures finished, when night approached Psyche went to bed; and when she was laid that the sweet sleep came upon her, she greatly feared, because she was alone: then came her unknown husband; and in the morning he rose before day, and departed.

Soon after came her invisible servants, presenting such things as were necessary. And thus she passed forth a great while; and as it happened the novelty of the things by continual custom did increase her pleasure, but specially the sound of the instruments was a comfort unto her being alone.

During this time that Psyche was in this place or pleasures her father and mother did nothing but weep and lament, and her two sisters, hearing of her most miserable fortune, came with great dolour and sorrow to comfort and speak with their parents.

The night following Psyche's husband spake unto her (for she might feel his eyes, his hands, and his ears), and said:

"O my sweet spouse and dear wife, fortune doth menace unto thee imminent peril and danger, whereof I wish thee greatly to beware. For know thou that thy sisters, thinking thou art dead, be greatly troubled, and are come to the mountain by thy steps. Whose lamentations if thou fortune to hear, beware that thou do in no wise either make

22

answer or look up towards them; for, if thou do, thou shalt purchase to me a great sorrow and to thyself utter destruction."

Psyche, hearing her husband, was contented to do all things as he commanded.

After that he was departed and the night passed away, Psyche lamented and cried all the day following, thinking that now she was past all hope of comfort, in that she was closed within the walls of a prison, deprived of human conversation, and commanded not to aid or assist her sorrowful sisters, no, nor once to see them.

Thus she passed all the day in weeping, and went to bed at night without any refection of meat or bain.

Incontinently after came her husband, who, when he had embraced her sweetly, gan say:

"Is it thus that you perform your promise, my sweet wife? What do I find here? Pass you all the day and the night in weeping, and will you not cease in your husband's arms? Go to; do what you will; purchase your own destruction; and, when find it so, then remember my words and repent, but too late."

Then she desired her husband more and more, assuring him that she should die unless he would grant that she might see her sisters, whereby she might speak with them and comfort them; whereat at length he was contented, and moreover he willed that she should give them as much gold and jewels as she would.

But he gave her a further charge, saying:

" Beware that ye covet not, being moved by the pernicious counsel of your sisters, to see the shape of my person, lest by your curiosity you be deprived of so great and worthy estate."

Psyche being glad herewith rendered unto him most entire thanks, and said:

"Sweet husband, I had rather die than to be separate from you; for, whosoever you be, I love and retain you within my heart as if you were mine own spirit or Cupid himself; but I pray you grant this likewise, that you would command your servant Zephyrus to bring my sisters down into the valley as he brought me."

Wherewithal she kissed him sweetly, and desired him gently to grant her request, calling him her spouse, her sweetheart, her joy, and her solace, whereby she enforced him to agree to her mind; and when morning came he departed away.

After long search made, the sisters of Psyche

came unto the hill where she was set on the rock, and cried with a loud voice in such sort that the stones answered again. And when they called their sister by her name, that their lamentable cries came unto her ears, she came forth, and said:

"Behold here is she for whom you weep; I pray you torment yourselves no more. Cease your weeping."

And by and by she commanded Zephyrus by the appointment of her husband to bring them down: neither did he delay, for with gentle blasts he retained them up, and laid them softly in the valley. I am not able to express the often embracing, kissing, and greeting, which was between them three; all sorrows and tears were then laid apart.

"Come in", quoth Psyche, "into our house, and refresh your afflicted minds with your sister."

After this she showed them the storehouses of treasure; she caused them to hear the voices which served her; the bain was ready; the meats were brought in; and, when they had eaten and filled themselves with divine delicacies, they conceived great envy within their hearts, and one of them being very curious did demand what her husband was, of what state and who was the Lord of so precious a house; but Psyche, remembering the promise which she made to her husband, feigned that he was a young man of comely stature, with a flaxen beard, and had great delight in hunting in the hills and dales by. And lest by her long talk she should be found to trip or fail in her words, she filled their laps with gold, silver, and jewels, and commanded Zephyrus to carry them away.

When they were brought up to the mountain,

they took their ways homeward to their own houses, and murmured with envy that they bare against Psyche, saying :

"Behold, cruel and contrary fortune, behold how we, born all of one parent, have divers destinies ; but especially we that are the elder two, be married to strange husbands, made as handmaidens, and as it were banished from our country and friends, whereas our youngest sister has so great abundance of treasure and gotten a God to her husband, who hath no skill how to use so great plenty of riches.

"Saw you not, sister, what was in the house, what great store of jewels, what glittering robes, what gems, what gold we trod on ? That if she have a husband according as she affirmeth, there is none that liveth this day more happy in all the world than she. And so it may come to pass that at length

for the great affection and love which he may bear
unto her, he may make her a Goddess; for, by
Hercules, such was her countenance, so she behaved
herself, that, as a Goddess, she had voices to serve
her and the winds did obey her. But I, poor wretch,
have first married a husband elder than my father,
more bald than a coot, more weak than a child, and
that locketh me up all day in the house."

Then said the other sister:

"And in faith I am married to a husband that
hath the gout, twyfold, crooked, not courageous in
paying my debt; I am fain to rub and mollify his
stony fingers with divers sorts of oils, and to wrap
them in plasters and salves, so that I soil my white
and dainty hands with the corruption of filthy clouts,
not using myself like a wife, but more like a servant.

"And you, my sister, seem likewise to be in

bondage and servitude, wherefore I cannot abide to see our younger sister in such great felicity. Saw you not, I pray, how proudly and arrogantly she handled us even now, and how in vaunting herself she uttered her presumptuous mind; how she cast a little gold into our laps; and, being weary of our company, commanded that we should be borne and blown away? Verily I live not nor am a woman but I will deprive her of all her bliss.

"And if you, my sister, be so far bent as I, let us consult together and not utter our mind to any person, no, nor yet to our parents, nor tell that ever we saw her. For it sufficeth that we have seen her whom it repenteth to have seen.

"Neither let us declare her good fortune to our father nor to any other, since, as they seem not happy whose riches are unknown, so shall she know that she hath sisters, no abjects, but more worthier than she.   But now let us go home to our husbands and poor houses, and, when we are better instructed, let us return to suppress her pride."

So this evil counsel pleased these two evil women, and they hid the treasure which Psyche gave them, and tore their hair, renewing their false and forged tears.   When their father and mother beheld them weep and lament still, they doubled their sorrows, and griefs; but, full of ire and forced with envy, they took their voyage homewards, devising the slaughter and destruction of their sister.

In the mean season the husband of Psyche did warn her again in the night with these words:

"Seest thou not", quoth he, "what peril and danger evil fortune doth threaten unto thee, whereof if thou take not good heed it will shortly come upon thee? For the unfaithful wretches do greatly endeavour to set their snares to catch thee, and their purpose is to make and persuade thee to behold my face, which if thou once fortune to see, as I have often told, thou shalt see no more.

"Wherefore if these naughty hags, armed with wicked minds, do chance to come again, as I think no otherwise but that they will, take heed that thou talk not with them, but simply suffer them to speak what they will.

"Howbeit if thou canst not restrain thyself, beware that thou have no communication of thy husband, nor answer a word if they fortune to question of me; so will we increase our stock, and our young and tender child, if thou conceal my secrets, shall be made an immortal god—otherwise a mortal creature."

32

Then Psyche was very glad that she should bring forth a divine babe, and very joyful in that she should be honoured as a mother.

But those pestilent and wicked furies, breathing out their serpentine poison, took shipping to bring their enterprise to pass. Then Psyche was warned again by her husband in this sort :

"Behold the last day, the extreme case, and the enemies of thy blood, hath armed themselves against us, pitched their camps, set their host in array, and are marching towards us, for now thy two sisters have drawn their swords and are ready to slay thee. Oh, with what force are we assailed this day !

"O sweet Psyche, I pray thee to take pity on thyself, of me; and deliver thy husband and this unborn infant from so great a danger; and see not, neither hear, these cursed women, which are not

C

worthy to be called thy sisters for their great hatred
and breach of sisterly amity; for they will come, like
sirens, to the mountain, and yield out their piteous
and lamentable cries."

When Psyche had heard these words, she sighed
sorrowfully, and said:

"O dear husband, this long time you have had
experience and trial of my faith, and doubt you not
but that I will persevere in the same; wherefore
command your wind Zephyrus that he may do as
he hath done before, to the intent that where you
have charged me not to behold your venerable face,
yet that I may comfort myself with the sight of my
sisters.

"I pray you, by these beautiful hairs, by these
round cheeks delicate and tender, by your pleasant
hot breast, whose shape and face I shall learn at

length by my child, grant the fruit of my desire;
refresh your dear spouse Psyche with joy, who is
bound and linked unto you for ever. I little esteem
to see your visage and figure—little do I regard the
night and darkness thereof, for you are my only
light."

Her husband, being as it were enchanted with
these words and compelled by violence of her often
embracing, wiping away her tears with his hair,
did yield unto his wife. And when morning came
departed as he accustomed to do.

Now her sisters arrived on land, and never rested
till they came to the rock, without visiting of their
father and mother, and leaped down rashly from the
hill themselves.

Then Zephyrus according to the divine commandment brought them down, though it were against

his will, and laid them in the valley without any harm.

By and by they went into the palace of their sister without leave, and, when they had eftsoons embraced their prey and thanked her with flattering words for the treasure which she gave them, they said:

"O dear sister Psyche, know you that you are now no more a child, but a mother: O what great joy bear you unto us! What a comfort will it be unto all the house! How happy shall we be that shall see this infant nourished amongst so great plenty of treasure, that if he be like his parents, as it is necessary he should, there is no doubt but a new Cupid shall be born."

By this kind of means they went about to win Psyche by little and little; but, because they were

36

weary with travel, they sat them down in chairs;
and, after that they had washed their bodies in bains,
they went into a parlour, where all kind of meats
were ready prepared.

Psyche commanded one to play with his harp;
it was done. Then immediately others sang; others
tuned their instruments; but no person was seen:
by whose sweet harmony and modulation the sisters
of Psyche were greatly delighted.

Howbeit the wickedness of these cursed women
was nothing suppressed by the sweet noise of these
instruments, but they settled themselves to work
their treason against Psyche, demanding who was
her husband, and of what parentage.

Then she, having forgotten by too much simplicity
that which she had spoken before of her husband,
invented a new answer, and said that her husband

37

was of a great province, a marchant, and a man of
middle age, having his beard intersparsed with grey
hairs, which when she had said, because she would
have no further talk, she filled their laps full of gold
and silver, and bid Zephyrus to bear them away.

In their return homeward they murmured with
themselves, saying :

"How say you, sister, to so apparent a lie of
Psyche's? For first she said that her husband was
a young man of flourishing years and had a flaxen
beard, and now she saith that it is half grey with
age : what is he that in so short space can become
so old? You shall find it no otherwise, my sister, but
that either this cursed queen hath invented a great
lie, or else that she never saw the shape of her
husband.

"And if it be so, that she never saw him, then
38

verily she is married to some God, and hath a young God in her bosom; but, if it be a divine babe and fortune to come to the ears of my mother (as God forbid it should), then may I go and hang myself; wherefore let us go to our parents, and with forged lies let us colour the matter."

After they were thus inflamed and had visited their parents, they returned again to the mountain, and by the aid of the wind Zephyrus were carried down into the valley; and, after they had strained their eyelids to enforce themselves to weep, they called unto Psyche in this sort:

"Thou, ignorant of so great evil, thinkest thyself sure and happy, and sittest at home nothing regarding thy peril, whereas we go about thy affairs, and are careful lest any harm should happen unto thee; for we are credibly informed, neither can we

but utter it unto thee, that there is a great serpent
full of deadly poison, with a ravenous and gaping
throat, that visiteth thee every night.

"Remember the oracle of Apollo, who pronounced
that thou shouldest be married to a dire and fierce
serpent; and many of the inhabitants hereby, and
such as hunt about in the country, affirm that they
saw him yester-night returning from pasture and
swimming over the river, whereby they do undoubtedly say that he will not pamper thee long
with delicate meats, but, when the time of delivery
shall approach, he will devour both thee and thy
child.

"Wherefore advise thyself whether thou wilt
agree unto us that are careful for thy safety, and
so avoid the peril of death, and be contented to
live with thy sisters, or whether thou wilt remain

with the serpent, and in the end to be swallowed into the gulf of his body. And if it be so that thy solitary life, thy conversation with voices, this servile and dangerous pleasure, and the love of the serpent, do more delight thee, say not but that we have played the parts of natural sisters in warning thee."

Then the poor simple miser Psyche was moved with the fear of so dreadful words, and, being amazed in her mind, did clean forget the admonitions of her husband and her own promises made unto him; and, throwing herself headlong into extreme misery, with a wan and sallow countenance, scantly uttering a third word, at length gan say in this sort:

"O my most dear sisters, I heartily thank you for your great kindness towards me, and I am now verily persuaded that they which you hear of have informed you of nothing but truth; for I never saw the shape of my husband, neither know I from whence he came; only I hear his voice in the night: insomuch that I have an uncertain husband and one that loveth not the light of the day, which causeth me to suspect that he is a beast, as you affirm. Moreover I do greatly fear to see him, for he doth menace and threaten great evil unto me, if I should go about to spy and behold his shape. Wherefore, my loving sisters, if you have any wholesome remedy for your sister in danger, give it now presently."

Then they, opening the gates of their subtle minds, did put away all privy guile, and egged her forward in her fearful thoughts, persuading her to do as they would have her; whereupon one of them began and said:

"Because that we little esteem any peril or

danger to save your life, we intend to show you the best way and mean as we may possibly do. Take a sharp razor and put it under the pillow of your bed, and see that you have ready a privy burning lamp with oil hid under some part of the hanging of the chamber; and, finely dissimulating the matter, when according to his custom he cometh to bed and sleepeth soundly, arise you secretly, and with your bare feet go and take your lamp, with the razor in your right hand, and with valiant force cut off the head of the poisonous serpent, wherein we will aid and assist you; and, when by the death of him you shall be made salve, we will marry you to some comely man."

After they had thus inflamed the heart of their sister, fearing lest some danger might happen unto them by reason of their evil counsel, they were carried by the wind Zephyrus to the top of the mountain, and so they ran away and took shipping.

When Psyche was left alone (saving that she seemed not to be alone, being stirred by so many furies), she was in a tossing mind like the waves of the sea ; and, although her will was obstinate and resisted to put in execution the counsel of her sisters, yet she was in doubtful and divers opinions touching her calamity. Sometime she would, sometime she would not ; sometime she is bold, sometime she feareth ; sometime she mistrusteth, sometime she is moved ; sometime she hateth the beast, sometime she loveth her husband : but at length the night came, whenas she made preparation for her wicked intent.

Soon after her husband came, and when he had kissed and embraced her, he fell asleep.

Then Psyche (somewhat feeble in body and mind, yet moved by cruelty of fate) received boldness, and brought forth the lamp, and took the razor—so by her audacity she changed her kind.

But, when she took the lamp and came to the bedside, she saw the most meek and sweetest beast of all beasts, even fair Cupid couched fairly, at whose sight the very lamp increased his light for joy, and the razor turned his edge. But when Psyche saw so glorious a body, she greatly feared, and, amazed in mind, with a pale countenance, all trembling, fell on her knees, and thought to hide the razor, yea verily in her own heart, which she had undoubtedly done, had it not through fear of so great an enterprise fallen out of her hand.

And, when she saw and beheld the beauty of his divine visage, she was well recreated in her mind.

She saw his hairs of gold that yielded out a sweet savour, his neck more white than milk, his purple cheeks, his hair hanging comely behind and before, the brightness whereof did darken the light of the lamp, his tender plume-feathers dispersed upon his shoulders like shining flowers and trembling hither and thither, and his other parts of his body so smooth and soft that it did not repent Venus to bear such a child.

At the bed's feet lay his bow, quiver, and arrows, that be the weapons of so great a God, which when Psyche did curiously behold, and, marvelling at the weapons of her husband, took one of the arrows out of the quiver, and pricked herself withal, wherewith she was so grievously wounded that the blood followed, and thereby of her own accord she added love upon love; then, more and more broiling in the

46

love of Cupid, she embraced him and kissed him
a thousand times fearing the measure of his
sleep.

But, alas, while she was in this great joy, whether
it were for envy or for desire to touch this amiable
body likewise, there fell out a drop of burning oil
from the lamp upon the right shoulder of the God.
O rash and bold lamp, the vile ministry of love, how
darest thou be so bold as to burn the God of all fire,
when he invented thee to the intent that all lovers
might with more joy pass the nights in pleasure?

The God being burned in this sort and perceiving
that promise and faith was broken, he fled away
without utterance of any word from the eyes and
hands of his most unhappy wife. But Psyche fortuned to catch him, as he was rising, by the right
thigh, and held him fast as he flew about in the

47

air, until such time that, constrained by weariness, she let go, and fell down upon the ground.

But Cupid followed her down, and lighted upon the top of a cypress tree, and angrily spake unto her in this manner:

"O simple Psyche, consider with thyself how I, little regarding the commandment of my mother, who willed me that thou shouldst be married to a man of base and miserable condition, did come myself from heaven to love thee, and wounded my own body with my proper weapons to have thee to my spouse. And did I seem a beast unto thee that thou shouldst go about to cut off my head with a razor who loved thee so well? Did not I always give thee in charge? Did not I gently will thee to beware? But those cursed aiders and counsellors of thine shall be worthily rewarded for

48

their pains. As for thee, thou shalt be sufficiently punished by my absence."

When he had spoken these words, he took his flight into the air.

Then Psyche fell flat on the ground, and as long as she might see her husband she cast her eyes after him into the air, weeping and lamenting piteously; but, when he was gone out of her sight, she threw herself into the next running river, for the great anguish and dolour that she was in, for the lack of her husband.

Howbeit the water would not suffer her to be drowned, but took pity upon her, in the honour of Cupid which accustomed to broil and burn the river, and so threw her upon the bank amongst the herbs.

Then Pan, the rustical God, sitting on the river-

side, embracing and teaching the Goddess Canna
to tune her songs and pipes, by whom were feeding
the young and tender goats, after that he perceived Psyche in so sorrowful case, not ignorant I
know not by what means of her miserable estate,
endeavoured to pacify her in this sort:

"O fair maid, I am a rustic and rude herdsman,
howbeit by reason of my old age expert in many
things; for, as far as I can learn by conjecture,
which, according as wise men do term, is called
divination, I perceive by your uncertain gait, your
pale hue, your sobbing sighs, and your watery eyes,
that you are greatly in love. Wherefore hearken
to me, and go not about to slay yourself, nor weep
not at all, but rather adore and worship the great
God Cupid, and win him unto you by your gentle
promise of service."

When the God of Shepherds had spoken these
words, she gave no answer, but made reverence
unto him as to a God, and so departed.

After that Psyche had gone a little way, she
fortuned unawares to come to a city where the
husband of one of her sisters did dwell; which,
when Psyche did understand, she caused that her
sister had knowledge of her coming, and so they
met together, and after great embracing and salu-
tation the sister of Psyche demanded the cause of
her travel thither.

"Marry", quoth she, "do not you remember
the counsel that you gave me, whereby you
would that I should kill the beast who under
colour of my husband visited me every night?
You shall understand that, as soon as I brought
forth the lamp to see and behold his shape, I

perceived that he was the son of Venus, even Cupid himself.

"Then I, being stroken with great pleasure and desirous to embrace him, could not thoroughly assuage my delight, but, alas! by evil chance the boiling oil of the lamp fortuned to fall on his shoulder, which caused him to awake, who, seeing me armed with fire and weapon, gan say: 'How darest thou be so bold as to do so great a mischief? Depart from me, and take such things as thou didst bring; for I will have thy sister (and named you) to my wife, and she shall be placed in my felicity.' And by and by he commanded Zephyrus to carry me away from the bounds of his house."

Psyche had scantly finished her tale but her sister, pierced with the prick of desire and wicked envy, ran home, and, feigning to her husband that she had heard of the death of her parents, took shipping, and came to the mountain. And, although there blew a contrary wind, yet, being brought in a vain hope, she cried:

"O Cupid, take me, a more worthy wife, and thou Zephyrus bear down thy mistress!" and so she cast herself down headlong from the mountain; but she fell not into the valley neither alive nor dead, for all the members and parts of her body were torn amongst the rocks, whereby she was made a prey to the birds and wild beasts, as she worthily deserved.

Neither was the vengeance of the other delayed; for Psyche travelling in that country fortuned to come to another city, where her other sister did dwell, to whom when she had declared all such things as she told to her first sister, she ran likewise unto the rock, and was slain in like sort.

Then Psyche travelled about in the country to seek her husband Cupid, but he was gotten into his mother's chamber, and there bewailed the sorrowful wound which he caught by the oil of the burning lamp.

Then the white bird, the Gull, which swimmeth on the waves of the water, flew towards the ocean sea, where she found Venus washing and bathing herself; to whom she declared that her son was burned and in danger of death; and moreover that it was a common bruit in the mouth of every person who spake evil of all the family of Venus that her son doth nothing but haunt wenches in the mountain, and she herself lasciviously used to

54

riot in the sea, whereby they say that they are now become no more gracious, no more pleasant, no more gentle, but incivil, monstrous, and horrible; moreover the marriages are not for any amity, or for love of pro-creation, but full of envy, discord, and debate.

This the curious Gull did clatter in the ears of Venus, reprehending her son. But Venus began to cry, and said:

"What, hath my son gotten any love? I pray thee, gentle bird, that dost serve me so faithfully, tell me what she is and what is her name that hath troubled my son in such sort — whether she be any of the Nymphs, of the number of the Goddesses, of the company of the Muses, or of the mistery of my Graces?"

To whom the bird answered:

55

"Madame, I know not what she is, but this I know, that she is called Psyche."

Then Venus with indignation cried out:

"What, is it she, the usurper of my beauty, the vicar of my name? What, will he think that I was a bawd, by whose show he fell acquainted with the maid?"

And immediately she departed and went to her chamber, where she found her son wounded, as it was told unto her, whom when she beheld she cried out in this sort:

"Is this an honest thing? Is this honourable to thy parents? Is this reason, that thou hast violated and broken the commandment of thy mother and sovereign mistress? And, whereas thou shouldst have vexed my enemy with loathsome love, thou hast done contrary; for, being but

56

of tender and unripe years, thou hast with too licentious appetite embraced my most mortal foe, to whom I shall be made a mother, and she a daughter.

"Thou presumest and thinkest, thou trifling boy, thou varlet and without all reverence, that thou art most worthy and excellent, and that I am not able by reason of mine age to have another son, which if I might have, thou shouldst well understand that I would bear a more worthier than thou.

"But to work thee a greater despite, I do determine to adopt one of my servants, and to give him these wings, this fire, this bow and these arrows, and all other furniture which I gave to thee not for this purpose, neither is anything given to thee of thy father for this intent; but first thou hast

57

been evil brought up and instructed in thy youth:
thou hast thy hands ready and sharp; thou hast
often offended thy ancients, and especially me that
am thy mother; thou hast pierced me with thy
darts, thou contemnest me as a widow, neither dost
thou regard thy valiant and invincible father; and
to anger me more thou art amorous of wenches.

"But I will cause that thou shalt shortly repent
thee, and that this marriage shall be dearly bought.
To what a point am I now driven?  What shall I
do?  Whither shall I go?  How shall I repress
this beast?  Shall I ask aid of mine enemy Sobriety,
whom I have often offended to engender thee?  Or
shall I seek for counsel of every poor and rustic
woman?  No, no, yet had I rather die; howbeit I
will not cease my vengeance; to her must I have
recourse for help, and to none other — I mean to

Sobriety, who may correct thee sharply, take away thy quiver, deprive thee of thine arrows, unbend thy bow, quench thy fire, and, which is more, subdue thy body with punishment; and when that I have rased and cut off this thy hair, which I have dressed with mine own hands and made to glitter like gold, and when I have clipped thy wings, which I myself have caused to burgen, then shall I think to have sufficiently revenged myself upon thee for the injury which thou hast done."

When she had spoken these words, she departed in a great rage out of her chamber.

Immediately as she was going away came Juno and Ceres, demanding the cause of her anger. Then Venus made answer:

"Verily you are come to comfort my sorrow, but I pray you with all diligence to seek out one whose name is Psyche, who is a vagabond, and runneth about the countries, and, as I think, you are not ignorant of the bruit of my son Cupid and of his demeanour, which I am ashamed to declare."

Then they, understanding and knowing the whole matter, endeavoured to mitigate the ire of Venus in this sort:

"What is the cause, madame, or how hath your son so offended, that you should so greatly accuse his love, and blame him by reason that he is amorous? And why should you seek the death of her whom he doth fancy?

"We most humbly entreat you to pardon his fault, if he have accorded to the mind of any maiden. What! Do not you know that he is a young man? Or have you forgotten of what years he is? Doth he seem always to you to be a child?

"You are his mother, and a kind woman—will you continually search out his dalliance? Will you blame his luxury? Will you bridle his love, and will you reprehend your own art and delights in him? What God or man is he that can endure that you should sow or disperse your seed of love in every place, and to make a restraint thereof within your own doors. Certes, you will be the cause of the suppression of the public places of young dames."

In this sort these Goddesses endeavoured to pacify her mind, and to excuse Cupid with all their power, although he were absent, for fear of his darts and shafts of love.

But Venus would in no wise assuage her heat;

but, thinking that they did but trifle and taunt at her injuries, she departed from them, and took her voyage towards the sea in all haste.

In the mean season Psyche hurled herself hither and thither, to seek for her husband; the rather because she thought that, if he would not be appeased with the sweet flattery of his wife, yet he would take mercy upon her at her servile and continual prayers. And, espying a church on the top of a high hill, she said:

"What can I tell whether my husband and master be there or no?"

Wherefore she went thitherward, and with great pain and travail, moved by hope, after that she climbed to the top of the mountain, she came to the temple, and went in: whereas, behold, she espied sheafs of corn lying on a heap, blades wreathed like garlands, and reeds of barley; more-over she saw hooks, scythes, sickles, and other instruments, to reap, but everything lay out of order and as it were cast in by the hands of labourers; which when Psyche saw, she gathered up, and put everything duly in order, thinking that she would not despise or contemn the Temples of any of the Gods, but rather get the favour and benevolence of them all.

By and by Ceres came in, and, beholding her busy and curious in her chapel, cried out afar off and said:

"O Psyche, needful of mercy, Venus searcheth for thee in every place to revenge herself and to punish thee grievously, but thou hast more mind to be here, and carest for nothing less than for thy safety."

Then Psyche fell on her knees before her,

watering her feet with her tears, wiping the ground with her hair, and with great weeping and lamentation desired pardon, saying:

"O great and holy Goddess, I pray thee by thy plenteous and liberal right hand, by thy joyful ceremonies of harvest, by the secrets of thy sacrifice, by the flying chariots of thy Dragons, by the tillage of the ground of Sicily which thou hast invented, by the marriage of Proserpina, by the diligent inquisition of thy daughter, and by the other secrets which are within the temple of Eleusis in the land of Athens, take pity on me thy servant Psyche, and let me hide myself a few days amongst these sheafs of corn until the ire of so great a Goddess be past, or until that I be refreshed of my great labour and travail."

Then answered Ceres:

"Verily, Psyche, I am greatly moved by thy prayers and tears, and desire with all my heart to aid thee; but, if I should suffer thee to be hidden here, I should incur the displeasure of my cousin, with whom I have made a treaty of peace and an ancient promise of amity: wherefore I advise thee to depart hence, and take it not in evil part in that I will not suffer thee to abide and remain within my temple."

Then Psyche, driven away contrary to her hope, was double afflicted with sorrow; and so she returned back again.

And, behold, she perceived afar off in a valley a temple standing within a forest, fair and curiously wrought; and, minding to overpass no place whither better hope did direct her and to the intent she would desire the pardon of every God, she

approached nigh to the sacred doors, whereas
she saw precious riches and vestments engraven
with letters of gold, hanging upon branches of
trees and the posts of the temple, testifying the
name of the Goddess Juno, to whom they were
dedicated.

Then she kneeled down upon her knees, and,
embracing the altar with her hands and wiping her
tears, gan pray in this sort:

"O dear spouse and sister of the great God
Jupiter, which art adored and worshipped among
the great temples of Samos, called upon by women
with child, worshipped at high Carthage, because
thou werest brought from heaven by the Lion, the
rivers of the flood Inachus do celebrate thee and
know that thou art the wife of the great God and
Goddess of Goddesses. All the East part of the

world hath thee in veneration; all the world calleth
thee Lucina: I pray thee to be mine advocate in
my tribulations; deliver me from the great danger
which pursueth me, and save me that am wearied
with so long labours and sorrow, for I know that
it is thou that succourest and helpest such women
as are with child and in danger."

Then Juno, hearing the prayers of Psyche,
appeared unto her in all her royalty, saying :

"Certes, Psyche, I would gladly help thee, but
I am ashamed to do anything contrary to the will
of my daughter-in-law Venus, whom always I have
loved as mine own child ; moreover I shall incur the
danger of the law intituled *De servo corrupto*,
whereby I am forbidden to retain any servant
fugitive against the will of his master."

Then Psyche, cast off likewise by Juno, as without all hope of the recovery of her husband reasoned with herself in this sort:

"Now what comfort or remedy is left to my afflictions, whenas my prayers will nothing avail with the Goddesses? What shall I do? Whither shall I go? In what cave or darkness shall I hide myself to avoid the furor of Venus? Why do I not take a good heart and offer myself with humility unto her whose anger I have wrought? What do I know whether he whom I seek for be in the house of his mother or no?"

Thus being in doubt, poor Psyche prepared herself to her own danger, and devised how she might make her orison and prayer unto Venus.

After that Venus was weary with searching by sea and land for Psyche, she returned toward heaven, and commanded that one should prepare her chariot, which her husband Vulcan gave unto her by reason of marriage, so finely wrought that neither gold nor silver could be compared to the brightness thereof. Four white pigeons guided the chariot with great diligence, and, when Venus was entered in, a number of sparrows flew chirping about, making sign of joy, and all other kind of birds sang sweetly for showing the coming of the great Goddess: the clouds gave place, the heavens opened and received her joyfully, the birds that followed nothing feared the eagles, hawks, and other ravenous fowl in the air.

Incontinently she went into the royal palace of the God Jupiter, and with proud and bold petition demanded the service of Mercury in certain of her affairs, whereunto Jupiter consented. Then with much joy she descended from Heaven with Mercury, and gave him an earnest charge to put in execution his words, saying:

"O my brother, born in Arcadia, thou knowest well that I (who am thy sister) did never enterprise to do anything without thy presence; thou knowest also how long I have sought for a girl and cannot find her, wherefore there resteth nothing else save that thou with thy trumpet do pronounce the reward to such as take her.  See thou put in execution my commandment, and declare that whatsoever he be that retaineth her wittingly against my will shall not defend himself by any mean or excusation."

Which when she had spoken, she delivered unto him a label wherein was contained the name of Psyche and the residue of his publication; which done, she departed away to her lodging.

By and by Mercury (not delaying the matter)

proclaimed throughout all the world that whatsoever he were that could tell any tidings of a King's fugitive daughter, the servant of Venus, named Psyche, should bring word to Mercury, and for reward of his pains he should receive seven sweet cosses[1] of Venus. After that Mercury had pronounced these things, every man was inflamed with desire to search out Psyche.

This proclamation was the cause that put away all doubt from Psyche, who was scantly come in sight of the house of Venus but one of her servants called Custom came out, who espying Psyche cried with a loud voice:

"O wicked wench as thou art, now at length thou shalt know that thou hast a mistress above thee. What! dost thou make thyself ignorant as thou

[1] Kisses.

didst not understand what travail we have taken in searching for thee? I am glad that thou art come into my hands; thou art now in the gulf of Hell, and shalt abide the pain and punishment of thy great contumacy."

And therewithal she took her by the hair, and brought her before the presence of the Goddess Venus.

When Venus espied her she began to laugh, and, as angry persons accustom to do, she shaked her head and scratched her right ear, saying:

"O Goddess, Goddess, you are now come at length to visit your mother, or else to see your husband that is in danger of death by your means— be you assured I will handle you like a daughter; where be my maidens Sorrow and Sadness?"

To whom, when they came, she delivered Psyche

to be cruelly tormented: then they fulfilled the commandment of their mistress, and, after they had piteously scourged her with whips and rods, they presented her again before Venus. Then she began to laugh again, saying :

"Behold she thinketh that by reason of her unborn child to move me to pity, and to make me a grandmother. Am not I happy that in the flourishing time of all mine age shall be called a grandmother, and the son of a vile wench shall be accounted the nephew of Venus? Howbeit I am a fool to term him by the name of son, since as the marriage was made between unequal persons, in the fields without witnesses and not by the consent of their parents, wherefore the marriage is illegitimate, and the child that shall be born a bastard, if we fortune to suffer thee to live till thou be delivered."

73

# Cupid and Psyche    ✦

When Venus had spoken these words she leaped upon the face of poor Psyche, and, tearing her apparel, took her violently by the hair, and dashed her head upon the ground. Then she took a great quantity of wheat, barley meal, poppy seed, peas, lentils, and beans, and mingled them all together on a heap, saying

"Thou evil-favoured girl, thou seemest unable to get the grace of thy lover by no other means but only by diligent and painful service, wherefore I will prove what thou canst do; see that thou separate all these grains one from another, disposing them orderly in their quality, and let it be done before night."

When she had appointed this task unto Psyche, she departed to a great banquet that was prepared that day.

74

But Psyche went not about to dissever the grain, as being a thing impossible to be brought to pass by reason it lay so confusedly scattered ; but, being astonished at the cruel commandment of Venus, sat still and said nothing.]

Then the little pismire the Emmet, taking pity of her great difficulty and labour, cursing the cruelness of the wife of Jupiter and of so evil a mother, ran about hither and thither, and called to her all the ants of the country, saying :

"I pray you, my friends, ye quick sons of the ground, the mother of all things, take mercy on this poor maid espoused to Cupid who is in great danger of her person. I pray you help her with all diligence."

Incontinently one came after another dissevering and dividing the grain ; and, after that they had put each kind of corn in order, they ran away again in all haste.

When night came, Venus returned home from the banquet well tippled with wine, smelling of balm, and crowned with garlands of roses, who, when she espied what Psyche had done, gan say :

"This is not the labour of thy hands, but rather of his that is amorous of thee."

Then she gave her a morsel of brown bread, and went to sleep.

In the mean season Cupid was closed fast in the most surest chamber of the house, partly because he should not hurt himself with wanton dalliance, and partly because he should not speak with his love : so these two lovers were divided one from another.

+ Cupid and Psyche

When night was passed, Venus called Psyche and said:

"Seest thou yonder forest that extendeth out in length with the river? There be great sheep shining like gold and kept by no manner of person: I command thee that thou go thither and bring me home some of the wool of their fleeces."

Psyche arose willingly, not to do her commandment but to throw herself headlong into the water to end her sorrow. Then a green reed, inspired by divine inspiration with a gracious tune and melody, gan say:

"O Psyche, I pray thee not to trouble or pollute my water with the death of thee, and yet beware that thou go not towards the terrible sheep of this coast, until such time as the heat of the sun be past; for, when the sun is in his force, then seem they most dreadful and furious with their sharp horns, their stony foreheads, and their gaping throats, wherewith they arm themselves to the danger of mankind; but until the midday is past and the heat assuaged, and until they have refreshed themselves in the river, thou mayst hide thyself here by me under this great plane tree; and, as soon as their great fury is past, thou mayst go among the thickets and bushes under the woodside, and gather the locks of their golden fleeces which thou shalt find hanging upon the briars."

Thus spake the gentle and benign reed, showing a mean to Psyche to save her life, which she bare well in memory, and with all diligence went and gathered up such locks as she found, and put them in her apron, and carried them home to Venus: howbeit the danger of this second labour did not please her, nor give her sufficient witness of the good service of Psyche, but with a sour resemblance of laughter, she said:

"Of certainty I know that this is not thy fact, but I will prove if thou be of so stout a courage and singular prudence as thou seemst."

Then Venus spake unto Psyche again, saying:

"Seest thou the top of yonder great hill from whence there runneth down water of black and deadly colour which nourisheth the floods of Styx and Cocytus? I charge thee to go thither and bring me a vessel of that water."

Wherewithal she gave her a bottle of crystal, menacing and threatening her rigorously.

Then poor Psyche went in all haste to the top of the mountain, rather to end her life than to fetch any water; and, when she was come up to

the ridge of the hill, she perceived that it was impossible to bring it to pass, for she saw a great
rock gushing out most horrible fountains of
waters, which ran down and fell by many stops
and passages into the valley beneath.

On each side she saw great dragons stretching
out their long and bloody necks that never slept,
but appointed to keep the river there; the waters
seemed to themselves likewise saying: .

"Away, away! what wilt thou do? Fly, fly!
or else thou wilt be slain."

Then Psyche, seeing the impossibility of this
affair, stood still as though she were trans-
formed into stone; and, although she was present
in body, yet was she absent in spirit and sense
by reason of the great peril which she saw; in
so much that she could not comfort herself with

weeping, such was the present danger she was in.

But the royal bird of great Jupiter, the Eagle, remembering his old service which he had done whenas by the prick of Cupid he brought up the boy Ganymede to the heavens to be made the butler of Jupiter, and minding to show the like service in the person of the wife of Cupid, came from the high house of the skies, and said unto Psyche :

"O simple woman without all experience, dost thou think to get or dip up any drop of this dreadful water ? No, no ! assure thyself that thou art never able to come nigh it, for the Gods themselves do greatly fear at the sight thereof. What ! have you not heard that it is a custom among men to swear by the puissance of the

F                                    81

Gods: And the Gods do swear by the majesty of the river Styx? But give me thy bottle."

And suddenly he took it and filled it with the water of the river, and, taking his flight through those cruel and horrible dragons, brought it unto Psyche, who, being very joyful thereof, presented it to Venus, who would not be appeased, but menacing more and more said:

"What! thou seemest unto me a very witch and enchantress that bringest these things to pass; howbeit thou shalt do one thing more. Take this box and go to Hell to Proserpina, and desire her to send me a little of her beauty, as much as will serve me the space of one day, and say that such as I had is consumed away since my son fell sick; but return again quickly, for I must dress myself therewithal and go to the theatre of the Gods."

Then poor Psyche perceived the end of all her fortune, thinking verily that she should never return, and not without cause, as she was compelled to go to the gulf and furies of Hell.

Wherefore without any further delay she went up to a high tower to throw herself down headlong, thinking that it was the next and readiest way to Hell, but the Tower, as inspired, spake unto her, saying:

"O poor miser, why goest thou about to slay thyself? Why dost thou rashly yield unto thy last peril and danger? Know thou that, if thy spirit be once separate from thy body, thou shalt surely go to Hell, but never to return again; wherefore hearken to me. Lacedaemon, a city of Greece, is not far hence.

"Go thou thither and inquire for the hill

Tænarus, whereas thou shalt find a hole leading
to Hell, even to the palace of Pluto; but take
heed that thou go not with empty hands to that
place of darkness, but carry two sops sodden in the
flour of barley and honey in thy hands, and two
halfpence in thy mouth; and, when thou hast
passed a good part of that way, thou shalt see a
lame Ass carrying of wood, and a lame fellow
driving him who will desire thee to give him up
the sticks that fall down; but pass thou on and
do nothing: by and by thou shalt come unto the
river of Hell, whereas Charon is ferryman, who
will first have his fare paid him before he will carry
the souls over the river in his boat. Whereby you
may see that avarice reigneth amongst the dead;
neither Charon nor Pluto will do anything for
naught. For, if it be a poor man that would pass

over and lacketh money, he shall be compelled to
die in his journey before they will show him any
relief.

"Wherefore deliver to carrion Charon one of the
halfpence which thou bearest for thy passage, and
let him receive it out of thy mouth. And it shall
come to pass as thou sittest in the boat thou shalt
see an old man swimming on the top of the river
holding up his deadly hands and desiring thee to
receive him into the bark, but have no regard to
his piteous cry. When thou art passed over the
flood, thou shalt espy old women spinning who
will desire thee to help them, but beware thou do
not consent unto them in any case, for these and
like baits and traps will Venus set to make thee
let fall one of thy sops; and think not that the
keeping of thy sops is a light matter, for if thou

lose one of them thou shalt be assured never to return again to this world.

"Then thou shalt see a great and marvellous dog with three heads, barking continually at the souls of such as enter in; by reason he can do them no other harm, he lieth day and night before the gate of Proserpina and keepeth the house of Pluto with great diligence, to whom if thou cast one of thy sops thou mayest have access to Proserpina without all danger. She will make you good cheer, and entertain thee with delicate meat and drink; but sit thou upon the ground and desire brown bread, and then declare thy message unto her; and, when thou hast received such beauty as she giveth, in thy return appease the rage of the dog with thy other sop, and give thy other halfpenny to covetous Charon, and come

the same way again into the world as thou
wentest.

"But above all things have a regard that thou
look not in the box, neither be not too curious
about the treasure of the divine beauty."

In this manner the Tower spake unto Psyche,
and advertized her what she should do; and immediately she took two halfpence, two sops, and
all things necessary, and went to the mountain
Tænarus to go towards Hell.

After that Psyche had passed by the lame ass,
paid her halfpenny for passage, neglected the old
man in the river, denied to help the women spinning, and filled the ravenous mouth of the dog with
a sop, she came to the chamber of Proserpina

There Psyche would not sit in any royal seat,
nor eat any delicate meats; but, kneeling at the

feet of Proserpina, only contented with coarse bread, declared her message; and, after she had received a mystical secret in the box, she departed, and stopped the mouth of the dog with the other sop, and paid the boatman the other halfpenny.

When Psyche was returned from Hell to the light of the world, she was ravished with great desire, saying:

"Am not I a fool that, knowing that I carry here the divine beauty, will not take a little thereof to garnish my face, to please my lover withal?"

And by and by she opened the box, where she could perceive no beauty nor anything else, save only an infernal and deadly sleep, which immediately invaded all her members, as soon as the box was uncovered, in such sort that she fell down on the ground and lay there as a sleeping corpse.

But Cupid, being now healed of his wound and malady, not able to endure the absence of Psyche, got him secretly out at a window of the chamber where he was enclosed, and receiving his wings, took his flight towards his loving wife; whom when he had found he wiped away the sleep from her face, and put it again into the box, and awaked her with the tip of one of his arrows, saying:

"O wretched caitiff, behold thou werest well-nigh perished again with thy overmuch curiosity; well, go thou, and do thy message to my mother, and in the mean season I will provide for all things accordingly."

Wherewithal he took his flight into the air, and Psyche brought her present to Venus.

Cupid being more and more in love with Psyche, and fearing the displeasure of his mother, did pierce into the heavens, and arrived before Jupiter to declare his cause.

Then Jupiter, after that he had eftsoons embraced him, gan say in this manner

"O my well-beloved son, although thou hast not given due reverence and honour unto me as thou oughtest to do, but hast rather soiled and wounded this my breast, whereby the laws and order of the elements and planets be disposed with continual assaults of terrene luxury and against all laws and the discipline Julia and the utility of the public weal, in transforming my divine beauty into serpents, fire, savage beasts, birds, and bulls.

"Howbeit, remembering my modesty and that I have nourished thee with mine own proper hands, I will do and accomplish all thy desire, so that thou canst beware of spiteful and envious persons.

And, if there be any excellent maiden of comely beauty in the world, remember yet the benefit which I shall show unto thee by recompense of her love towards me again."

When he had spoken these words, he commanded Mercury to call all the Gods to council, and if any of the celestial powers did fail of appearance he should be condemned in ten thousand pounds; which sentence was such a terror unto all the Gods that the high theatre was replenished, and Jupiter began to speak in this sort:

"O ye Gods, registered in the books of the Muses, you all know this young man Cupid, whom I have nourished with mine own hands, whose raging flames of his first youth I thought best to bridle and restrain. It sufficeth in that he is defamed in every place for his riotous living, wherefore all occasion ought to be taken away by means of marriage: he hath chosen a maiden that fancieth him well; let him have her still and possess her according to his own pleasure."

Then he returned to Venus, and said:

"And you, my daughter, take you no care, neither fear the dishonour of your progeny and estate, neither have regard in that it is a mortal marriage, for it seemeth unto me just, lawful, and legitimate by the law civil."

Incontinently after, Jupiter commanded Mercury to bring up Psyche, the spouse of Cupid, into the palace of heaven. And then he took a pot of immortality, and said:

"Hold, Psyche, and drink to the end thou mayst be immortal, and that Cupid may be thine everlasting husband."

92

## + Cupid and Psyche

By and by the great banquet and marriage-feast was sumptuously prepared. Cupid sat down with his dear spouse between his arms; Juno likewise with Jupiter; and all the other Gods in order. Ganymede filled the pot of Jupiter, and Bacchus served the rest.

Their drink was nectar, the wine of the Gods. Vulcan prepared supper, the Hours decked up the house with roses and other sweet smells, the Graces threw about balm, the Muses sang with sweet harmony, Apollo tuned pleasantly to the harp, Venus danced finely, Satyr and Pan played on their pipes; and thus Psyche was married to Cupid, and after she was delivered of a child, whom we call Pleasure.